Frog or Toad?

Written by Sue Barraclough

Collins

Is a frog the same as a toad?

Frogs and toads lay eggs in ponds or streams. Toads lay eggs in a long string. Frogs lay eggs in a big clump.

toad eggs

frog eggs

2

Frog and toad eggs grow bigger.
They grow into tadpoles.
They look like little fish.

frog tadpole

3

Most toad tadpoles are darker
and smaller than frog tadpoles.
Growing tadpoles feed on weeds.
As a tadpole gets bigger
it grows legs.

toad tadpole

legs

4

When a tadpole
grows bigger
it has no tail.
Tadpoles grow
into little frogs
and toads.
Now they can
hop out of
the pond
to feed.

little frog

little toad

All frogs have long back legs.
Long legs help frogs to hop and swim fast.
Frogs have webbed feet to help them swim.

webbed feet

A toad's legs are not as long.
Toads are slow and do not swim as much.
Toads stay still and hide.

A frog has skin that is wet and smooth. Its wet skin shines. A frog's skin can be bright green, yellow or blue.

A toad has skin that is dry with bumps.
Its dry skin has no shine. A toad's skin is dull.

Frogs and toads eat
the same food.
They like to eat lots
of slugs and bugs.

Frogs and toads feed on spiders and flies. When a toad sees a fly it can eat, it plucks the fly up.

Other animals can attack or eat frogs and toads. Frogs can make loud sounds. Some frogs croak. Some frogs scream when they get a fright.

Some toads puff up when they get a shock.
They try to look bigger to make other
animals go away.

13

A frog

wet skin that shines

lays eggs in a clump

long legs with webbed feet

croaks and screams when scared

likes to hop and swim

A toad

lays eggs in a string

dry skin with bumps

shorter legs than a frog

puffs up when scared

likes to stay still and hide

15

Ideas for reading

Written by Clare Dowdall, PhD
Lecturer and Primary Literacy Consultant

Learning objectives: recognise and use alternative ways of pronouncing the graphemes already taught; recognise automatically an increasing number of familiar high frequency words; apply phonic knowledge and skills as the prime approach to reading unfamiliar words that are not completely decodable; find specific information in simple texts

Curriculum links: Science – Life processes and living things

Focus phonemes: ay, ie, ea, ue, a-e, i-e, u-e

Fast words: like, little, they, have, when

Word count: 324

Getting started

- Revise sound-talking some CCVC and CCVCC words, e.g. *f-r-o-g*; *c-l-u-m-p*, preparing children for reading them in the book.

- Invite children to add sound buttons to some longer words with adjacent consonants, e.g. *s-t-r-ea-m-s*; *s-t-r-i-ng*.

- Read the title and blurb together. Discuss who has seen a frog or a toad and whether they know what the difference is between them.

Reading and responding

- Ask children to read the book from the beginning to the end, taking time to look at the pictures to help make meaning.

- Move around the group, listening to them blending through words independently, praising their blending.

- Support children to read more complex words using phonic knowledge.

- Invite fast finishers to reread the book, collecting three facts about the differences between frogs and toads.